THIS BLOOMSBURY BOOK

BELONGS TO

....

KIDOGO

OKAPI

GIRAFFE

RHINOCEROS

BONGO   KIDOGO'S MAMA

LION   HIPPOPOTAMUS   SHOEBILL   LEOPARD

KIDOGO

For Noel, my own Kidogo

Note: The word *kidogo* means *little* in Kiswahili. It is pronounced Kee-doe-go.
Kidogo kidogo means *little by little*.

First published in Great Britain in 2005 by Bloomsbury Publishing Plc,
36 Soho Square, London, W1D 3QY
This paperback edition first published in 2006
First Published in the United States of America by Bloomsbury Children's Books USA, New York
Text and illustrations copyright © Anik McGrory 2005
Typeset in TLPierre Bonnard and Cooper Old Style Light.
The art was created with pencil and watercolour.
The moral right of the author/illustrator has been asserted
A CIP catalogue record of this book is available from the British Library
ISBN 0 7475 7635 1
9780747576358
Printed and bound in Singapore by Tien Wah Press
1 3 5 7 9 10 8 6 4 2
All papers used by Bloomsbury Publishing are natural, recyclable products
made from wood grown in well-managed forests. The manufacturing processes
conform to the environmental regulations of the country of origin.

KIDOGO

ANIK McGRORY

BLOOMSBURY
CHILDREN'S
BOOKS

Kidogo lived in a world that was vast.
He walked under a mountain bigger than the clouds.

He played on endless fields of rippling gold.

And he slept through nights that
were deeper than his dreams.

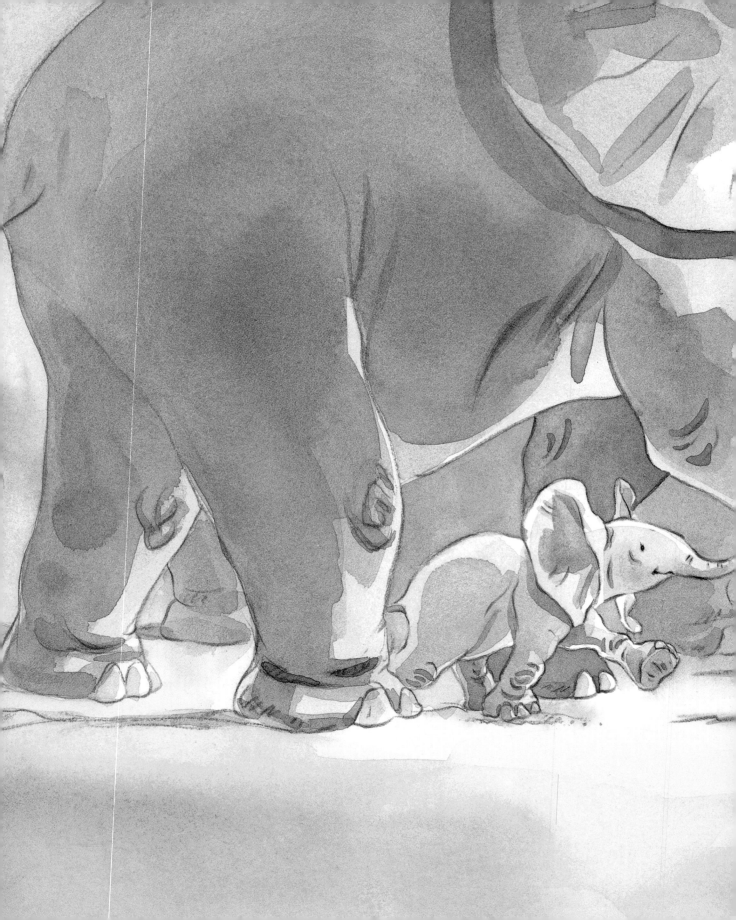

He was very small...for an elephant.

His aunties helped
him reach tender
acacia leaves.

His cousins helped him cross
the flooding river.

His mama helped him with his dust bath,
although he wasn't sure he needed one.

But Kidogo didn't want help.
He didn't want to be the smallest.
So he went off to find someone in the world
who was just as small as he.

He looked in the woodlands.

He looked in the flooding river.

He looked on the plains.

He looked until he knew it was true...

...he was the smallest animal in all the world.

He stopped, lost and alone,
with no place left to look.

He sat and decided.

He wouldn't need anyone else—
big or small.

He would find his own
acacia leaves.

He would cross the river by himself.

He would make his own dust bath.
But as the dust fell around him,
there was a tickling and an itching on
his ears and tail and legs and nose.

He swiped and rolled

and brushed

and blew...

...until, finally, the itching stopped.
And there, as he looked down,
was an animal smaller than
he had ever imagined.
Soon he was
surrounded by
tiny animals.

He helped them reach tender acacia leaves.

He helped them cross a flooding river.

He helped them with a dust bath,
although they weren't sure they needed one.

He followed the insects on a march down
the riverbank, through the woodlands,
across the plains, and back to his very own home.

Kidogo saw the insects and the mountains,
little and big. There were his cousins,
his aunties, and his mama.

And Kidogo knew he wasn't too small after all.

He was just right...for a little elephant.

About Elephants

An African baby elephant lives with its extended family. Big sisters and aunties often act as babysitters, keeping him out of mischief and standing watch while he sleeps at their feet. When a little one is upset or frightened, everyone helps to comfort him. When a boy elephant grows up he will move off to live with a group of other males. A girl elephant will stay with her family for her whole life.

Elephants can talk with each other! They make a special low frequency sound that people cannot hear. But other elephants can hear this sound from almost ten kilometres away. This is how elephant families communicate when they are apart. They can warn each other of danger or arrange to meet. People can only detect these noises using special equipment.

All elephants love to play, flapping their ears, lifting their tails and trumpeting. Bigger cousins will lie down to let the babies tumble on top of them. They like nothing better than a new toy – a funny stick or a swishy palm leaf – that they can roll with their feet and swing with their trunks. Elephants even smile!

Elephants are affectionate animals, cuddling with their trunks and reassuring each other with deep rumbling sounds. When meeting a long lost friend, elephants click tusks and wrap their trunks together.

Jamaa means 'family' in Kiswahili. *Kusema* is the Kiswahili word for 'talk'. *Kucheza* is the word for 'play'. *Upendo* means 'love'.

Tembo is the Kiswahili word for 'elephant'.

Kiswahili is spoken in many African countries where elephants can also be found.

BUTTERFLY   HORNBILL   JACKAL   VERVET MONKEY   DIK-DIK

KIDOGO   ANT   TERMITE   HYRAX   ELEPHANT SHREW   HOO

KINGFISHER   BEE-EATERS

H BABY   KLIPSPRINGER   BABOON   THOMSON'S GAZELLE

Enjoy more fabulous books from Bloomsbury Children's Books . . .

Tea With Bea
Louis Baum and Georgie Birkett

Looking After Little Ellie
Dosh and Mike Archer

Ten Little Sleepyheads
Elizabeth Provost and Donald Saaf

Beep Beep, Let's Go!
Eleanor Taylor

Available in paperback